Copyright © 1996 by Nord-Süd Verlag AG, Gossau Zürich, Switzerland
First published in Switzerland under the title *Marie reist ins Schachtelland*
English translation copyright © 1996 by North-South Books Inc.

All rights reserved. No part of this book may be reproduced or utilized
in any form or by any means, electronic or mechanical, including photocopying,
recording, or any information storage and retrieval system,
without permission in writing from the publisher.

First published in the United States, Great Britain, Canada,
Australia, and New Zealand in 1996 by North-South Books,
an imprint of Nord-Süd Verlag AG, Gossau Zürich, Switzerland.

Distributed in the United States by North-South Books Inc., New York.

Library of Congress Cataloging-in-Publication Data is available.
A CIP catalogue record for this book is available from The British Library.
ISBN 1-55858-539-7 (trade binding)
1 3 5 7 9 TB 10 8 6 4 2
ISBN 1-55858-540-0 (library binding)
1 3 5 7 9 LB 10 8 6 4 2
Printed in Belgium

A Princess in Boxland

BY TANJA SZÉKESSY

Translated by J. Alison James

NORTH-SOUTH BOOKS / NEW YORK / LONDON

Marie was a princess.
She didn't look like your ordinary fairy-tale princess,
with long, wavy hair and sea-blue eyes.
She didn't even have fancy princess clothes.
But all the same, she knew she was a princess
because of the unusual things that happened to her.

Like the day she found the red umbrella . . .

and snapped it open, and clicked it shut,
and took it with her into the box,

where she tumbled into . . .

BOXLAND!

"Welcome!" squawked the bird.

The gardener watered

a stream to the sea . . .

and gave her a paper hat and a boat.

And Marie sailed like a princess over sea-blue waves.

But paper boats can't keep out water
the way umbrellas can.

A little shaken and not quite dry,
Marie still managed to curtsy
to the king and queen of Boxland.

"You must be hungry, dear," they said.
But suddenly . . .

. . . rumpledee pumpledee plump!
Marie tumbled down a cascade of apples,
which woke the royal lion, who started to roar.

But because she was a princess,
Marie knew how to handle royal lions.

A sweet apple between the jaws
and an umbrella in the claws.
"Looks like rain," Marie said. "Must dash!"

And she clambered over boxes full of adventures
she'd never even dreamed of, because . . .

even a *princess*
has to get home on time.